THE BOXCAR CHILDREN MYSTERIES

THE BOXCAR CHILDREN
SURPRISE ISLAND
THE YELLOW HOUSE MYSTERY
MYSTERY RANCH
MIKE'S MYSTERY
BLUE BAY MYSTERY
THE WOODSHED MYSTERY
THE LIGHTHOUSE MYSTERY
MOUNTAIN TOP MYSTERY
SCHOOLHOUSE MYSTERY
CABOOSE MYSTERY
HOUSEBOAT MYSTERY
SNOWBOUND MYSTERY
TREE HOUSE MYSTERY
BICYCLE MYSTERY
MYSTERY IN THE SAND
MYSTERY BEHIND THE WALL
BUS STATION MYSTERY
BENNY UNCOVERS A MYSTERY
THE HAUNTED CABIN MYSTERY
THE DESERTED LIBRARY MYSTERY
THE ANIMAL SHELTER MYSTERY
THE OLD MOTEL MYSTERY
THE MYSTERY OF THE HIDDEN PAINTING
THE AMUSEMENT PARK MYSTERY
THE MYSTERY OF THE MIXED-UP ZOO
THE CAMP-OUT MYSTERY
THE MYSTERY GIRL
THE MYSTERY CRUISE
THE DISAPPEARING FRIEND MYSTERY
THE MYSTERY OF THE SINGING GHOST
THE MYSTERY IN THE SNOW
THE PIZZA MYSTERY
THE MYSTERY HORSE
THE MYSTERY AT THE DOG SHOW
THE CASTLE MYSTERY
THE MYSTERY OF THE LOST VILLAGE
THE MYSTERY ON THE ICE
THE MYSTERY OF THE PURPLE POOL
THE GHOST SHIP MYSTERY
THE MYSTERY IN WASHINGTON, DC
THE CANOE TRIP MYSTERY
THE MYSTERY OF THE HIDDEN BEACH
THE MYSTERY OF THE MISSING CAT
THE MYSTERY AT SNOWFLAKE INN

THE MYSTERY ON STAGE
THE DINOSAUR MYSTERY
THE MYSTERY OF THE STOLEN MUSIC
THE MYSTERY AT THE BALL PARK
THE CHOCOLATE SUNDAE MYSTERY
THE MYSTERY OF THE HOT AIR BALLOON
THE MYSTERY BOOKSTORE
THE PILGRIM VILLAGE MYSTERY
THE MYSTERY OF THE STOLEN BOXCAR
THE MYSTERY IN THE CAVE
THE MYSTERY ON THE TRAIN
THE MYSTERY AT THE FAIR
THE MYSTERY OF THE LOST MINE
THE GUIDE DOG MYSTERY
THE HURRICANE MYSTERY
THE PET SHOP MYSTERY
THE MYSTERY OF THE SECRET MESSAGE
THE FIREHOUSE MYSTERY
THE MYSTERY IN SAN FRANCISCO
THE NIAGARA FALLS MYSTERY
THE MYSTERY AT THE ALAMO
THE OUTER SPACE MYSTERY
THE SOCCER MYSTERY
THE MYSTERY IN THE OLD ATTIC
THE GROWLING BEAR MYSTERY
THE MYSTERY OF THE LAKE MONSTER
THE MYSTERY AT PEACOCK HALL
THE WINDY CITY MYSTERY
THE BLACK PEARL MYSTERY
THE CEREAL BOX MYSTERY
THE PANTHER MYSTERY
THE MYSTERY OF THE QUEEN'S JEWELS
THE STOLEN SWORD MYSTERY
THE BASKETBALL MYSTERY
THE MOVIE STAR MYSTERY
THE MYSTERY OF THE PIRATE'S MAP
THE GHOST TOWN MYSTERY
THE MYSTERY OF THE BLACK RAVEN
THE MYSTERY IN THE MALL
THE MYSTERY IN NEW YORK
THE GYMNASTICS MYSTERY
THE POISON FROG MYSTERY
THE MYSTERY OF THE EMPTY SAFE
THE HOME RUN MYSTERY
THE GREAT BICYCLE RACE MYSTERY

THE BOXCAR CHILDREN®

CREATED BY
GERTRUDE CHANDLER WARNER

BOOK
156

THE SKELETON KEY MYSTERY

ILLUSTRATED BY
ANTHONY VanARSDALE

ALBERT WHITMAN & COMPANY
CHICAGO, ILLINOIS

Printed in the United States of America
10 9 8 7 6 5 4 3 2 1 LB 24 23 22 21 20

Illustrations by Anthony VanArsdale

Visit The Boxcar Children® online at www.boxcarchildren.com.
For more information about Albert Whitman & Company,
visit our website at www.albertwhitman.com.

Contents

Time Is Running Out!

"'I run all day and never walk. I tell you something, but I don't talk.'" Benny Alden slowly sounded out each word on the piece of paper.

"Good job, Benny," said Jessie. She was twelve and knew how much her six-year-old brother loved learning to read.

Violet snapped a picture of the page with her camera. Violet was ten, and she always photographed the children's adventures—even the spooky ones. "Now we just have to figure out what it means," she said.

"Something that runs without walking...and tells us something without talking. Those are clues," said Henry. At fourteen, he was the oldest of the Alden children. He liked solving problems. "The answer must be hidden somewhere in this room."

Benny looked around with his flashlight. The room had once been a study. But it seemed as though no one had used it in years. There was a clutter of old objects. And plenty of cobwebs. The single window had been painted over, and the only light came from a dim lamp in a corner. In the opposite corner, a wooden box shaped like a coffin leaned against the wall.

Violet searched along a shelf stuffed with old books and trinkets. "There are so many places for things to hide," she said. "The answer to the riddle could be anywhere."

Suddenly, Violet jumped. Out of the corner of her eye, she had seen something move.

"Are you okay?" Jessie asked.

Violet turned and let out a sigh of relief. In a large, dusty mirror, she saw her reflection looking back at her. "Yes," she said. "This room is full of surprises."

Jessie looked up at the strange clock on the wall. It was a made of metal and shaped like a skull. "We only have ten minutes left," she said. "We need to hurry!"

"Oh!" said Henry.

"What is it?" asked Violet. "Did something happen?"

Henry shined his light toward the strange clock. "I think I figured out the riddle," he said. "Something that runs and never walks..."

It took Jessie a moment. Then she understood. "A clock runs but never walks!" she said. "And it tells us the time without saying a word!"

The children gathered around the strange clock. Its eyes glowed red. Cobwebs hung from all sides.

"It's too high to reach," said Violet. "Even for you, Henry."

"Benny, come sit on my shoulders," Henry said.

Benny looked up at the clock and gulped. "Are—are you sure that's the answer to the clue?" he asked.

"I'm sure," said Henry. "Come on. Let's check it out."

Benny climbed onto Henry's shoulders, and Henry lifted him up to the clock.

"I don't see anything," said Benny.

"Feel inside the mouth," said Henry. "There could be something in there."

"The mouth?!" said Benny. "What if it tries to bite me?"

"The skull isn't alive," said Henry. "It can't bite you."

Benny closed his eyes and looked away. Slowly, he reached his fingers into the clock. Then he yanked his hand away and squealed.

"What is it?" asked Jessie.

"It felt like a tooth!" said Benny.

"Benny, we need to hurry," said Violet.

"Okay, I'll grab it this time." Benny reached back in, quickly this time, and pulled out a small flashlight. He turned it on, and a purple glow appeared.

"A purple light!" cried Violet. "How pretty!" Violet loved the color purple. She had purple ribbons tied on her pigtails and was wearing purple sneakers.

Benny handed the flashlight to Henry.

"This is called a black light," said Henry. "Black lights can show things that are fluorescent."

"What in the world does that mean?" asked Violet.

"Things that are fluorescent absorb ultraviolet light," said Jessie. "It makes them glow."

"So some things might glow if we point the black light at them?" asked Violet.

"That's right," said Henry. "Benny, reach back in there. Maybe there is a clue about the black light."

Benny sighed and reached into the skull's mouth once more. This time, he pulled out a folded piece of paper and handed it to Jessie. Henry lowered him to the floor.

"That was very brave," said Jessie. "Because you faced your fears, we found two clues to help us get out of here."

"Fears?" said Benny, blushing. "I wasn't afraid. I just—I didn't want to upset the cobwebs."

Jessie smiled at her little brother. She quickly unfolded the paper and handed it to him. "Well, either way, you get to tell us what the next clue says."

Benny sounded out the words on the page. "'I'm like a garden of blossoms bright. That only blooms in dark of night.'"

"I wonder what that could be," said Violet.

The Aldens shined their lights around the room, and Henry started listing what he saw. "There are books, an old lamp, a desk, a vase—"

"A coffin," said Benny, turning back to the big box in the corner. "And there's probably a skeleton inside of that."

"Oh Benny, don't let your imagination get the best of you," said Jessie. "It's just for show. There's nothing inside." Jessie knocked on the box to prove that it was hollow, but Benny still wasn't so sure.

"I have an idea," said Violet. "What if the answer is flowers?"

"Good thinking, Violet," said Henry. "Let's turn off our flashlights and see if the flowers in the vase shine in the black light."

Benny was still eyeing the coffin in the corner of the room. "Are you sure we have to turn off our lights?" he said. "Maybe it's not the flowers after all."

"It will be fine," said Jessie. She grabbed Benny's hand, and all the children shut off their lights. Henry held up the black light to the vase.

"It's all dark." Violet frowned. "No bright blooms anywhere."

"Maybe we should turn our flashlights back on and think some more," said Benny.

"Let's look around the room first," said Jessie, squeezing Benny's hand. "According to the clue, something should be glowing."

The children looked all around. Violet was the first to look up. "There are stars on the ceiling!" she said.

Sure enough, with the black light, the ceiling was glowing like the night sky.

"A garden that blooms at night—stars!" said Jessie. "Good eyes, Violet."

Henry panned the light across the ceiling. "They must be made of some kind of special paint," he said.

"We need to figure out what the clue means," said Jessie. "We only have a few minutes before we're stuck in here!"

Henry studied the glowing stars. With his finger, he traced the shape that the brightest ones made. "It's like a constellation," he said.

"What's that?" asked Benny.

"A constellation is a shape made by the brightest stars," Jessie explained.

Benny tilted his head. "Oh, I see. It looks like the letter T!"

"Does that mean we need to look for something that starts with that letter?" asked Violet. She studied the room. "T could stand for *table, tray, teacup, typewriter*. Now that I think of it, there are a lot of things that start with *T*."

Henry squinted at the shape. "I don't think it's a T. I think it's an arrow!"

Benny clicked on his light and guided it along the arrow and across the room. The beam came to rest on the coffin in the corner. "I knew there was something in there!" he said. Benny stepped behind Jessie.

The other children turned on their flashlights and pointed them at the wooden box. Slowly, Henry walked over. As he pulled on the cover, the hinges gave an eerie creak. Finally, Henry yanked open the cover and shined his flashlight inside.

"There's nothing here!" he said.

"See, Benny? Nothing to worry about," said Jessie.

Time Is Running Out!

"Except we need to figure out how to get out of here!" said Violet. "We don't have much time left."

Henry, Jessie, and Violet searched around the old coffin. The inside was smooth and lined with silk. Henry felt along the edges. "I don't feel anything hidden inside," he said.

"Maybe we misread the clue," said Jessie.

Benny was still standing away from the coffin. He noticed something on the open cover. "There's a pocket!" he said.

Jessie looked at the lid, where there was a small pouch. "Good eyes, Benny," she said, reaching inside.

"Hurry!" said Benny, wringing his hands. "We have less than a minute to get out!"

"There's something in here!" said Jessie. She pulled out a long, metal object with a fancy-looking handle.

"It's the skeleton key!" Benny cried.

The children ran to the entrance. Jessie jiggled the key into the lock, and the heavy door swung open. The Aldens rushed out as the room went black.

***

"Just in time!" said a tall man standing on the other side of the door. James Alden smiled at his four grandchildren.

"I'll say!" said Henry. "That was a close call!"

"Your grandchildren are indeed terrific mystery solvers, James! Just as you described them." Verónica applauded along with her daughter, Maru.

Verónica was a friend of Grandfather's. The Aldens were staying with her and Maru as they visited the town of Hammond Hills. It was October in the Northeast, and the rolling hills of Appalachia were alive with the bright colors of autumn. People had come from miles around to look at the brilliant leaves and enjoy fall activities.

"I'm glad you were able to solve my escape room!" said Maru. "Were the riddles hard to figure out?"

"The riddles were very clever," said Jessie.

"But we all worked together to solve them," said Violet.

"I was the clue reader!" said Benny, smiling proudly.

Henry nodded.

"We used to live in one room," said Henry. "And we escaped from it as well!"

The Aldens all laughed at the joke about how they had met Grandfather.

After their parents died, the four children had run away. For a little while, they had lived in a boxcar in the woods. At the time, they thought their grandfather was mean. But when James Alden finally found them, the children discovered he wasn't mean at all. He brought the children and their dog, Watch, to live with him in Greenfield, Connecticut. Grandfather even put the boxcar in the backyard to be the children's playhouse.

"Thank you, all, for being my test group," said Maru. "I worked late nights getting that room ready. Now I need to get back to work on these decorations. I want everything to be perfect for the grand opening tomorrow." Maru looked out the front window and then glanced at her watch. "Where is that Nick? He was supposed to be here an hour ago."

"Who is Nick?" asked Henry.

"He works for me, or at least he's supposed

to," said Maru. "He's full of good ideas, but I am starting to think he's not that dependable."

"We can help you with the decorations," said Jessie. "We've decorated for Halloween lots of times!"

The children all nodded. They liked to help.

"That's very kind," said Maru. "Thank you."

"James and I will head to the house and see about getting dinner ready," said Verónica.

"Oh, good," said Benny. "Puzzle solving makes me hungry!"

Jessie chuckled at her always-hungry little brother.

After Grandfather and Verónica had left, Maru said, "Let's start by opening those boxes by the door."

The Skeleton Key Mystery Room was in an old house. Besides the escape room, the main floor had a living room and a dining room, which had been turned into a lobby. On the second floor was storage and Maru's office.

"This is a beautiful lobby," said Violet, looking around the bright room filled with antiques.

"Thank you," Maru said. "When I bought this little house, there wasn't much in it. I've collected furniture and other items from rummage sales and secondhand stores."

"What gave you the idea to turn the house into an escape room?" asked Jessie.

"I moved back here to be closer to Mom," said Maru. "And with so many people coming to town during the fall season, I thought a Halloween-themed business would be perfect. I've always loved haunted houses, but an escape room seemed like something new and different!"

"We sure enjoyed it," said Henry.

"That's right," said Jessie. "We like solving mysteries."

The children helped Maru decorate. They unpacked strings of lights shaped like bones, bats, and skulls. Henry and Jessie started to string the lights across the lobby.

"I'll hang up these flying skeleton banners," said Violet. She held up a plastic skeleton with a flowing black robe. "And I'll put this one at the piano, like he's playing."

"Good idea!" said Maru. She handed Violet a roll of tape.

"I can put candy in these bowls," said Benny. He held up a handful of wrapped candy bars.

"Thank you, Benny," said Maru. "But no tasting before dinner!" she added with a chuckle.

Benny placed the candy into bowls shaped like ghosts. He imagined the wide-mouthed ghosts were hungry for candy bars and smiled.

Benny placed a bowl on the desk by the front door and another on the table between two chairs. A third bowl went on the piano. He placed the fourth on a table next to the back door.

The old house felt cozier with decorations. For the first time, Benny started to relax. Then he peeked out the window into the backyard. It was just getting dark, and a mist was moving in. An iron fence ran along the back of the yard, with a big iron gate in the middle. Beyond the gate, Benny saw rows of worn stones covered by twisting vines. "Is...is that a graveyard?" he asked.

"Oh, yes. Didn't I tell you?" Maru smirked. "Makes the Skeleton Key a little spookier, doesn't it?"

The Skeleton Key Mystery

Benny was about to say that he was too old to be afraid of graveyards. But before he could open his mouth, the iron gate in the yard slowly began to swing open.

A Visit in the Night

Benny stared as two glowing yellow eyes appeared at the gate, surrounded in fog. The eyes moved closer, revealing a dark face with snarling teeth and pointed ears that looked like horns. Behind the creature a tall, pale figure appeared out of the mist, lurching forward from among the gravestones.

"There's a horned monster and a walking skeleton out there!" Benny yelled, running from the window and grabbing Jessie's hand.

Henry raced to the back door with Maru close behind.

"Oh, Benny, that's just Burke and his dog, Hannibal," Maru said. "Burke is the graveyard caretaker. He lives in a little cottage on the other side of the property."

"Benny, I think that imagination of yours is working hard again," said Jessie.

"I don't know," said Violet, peeking shyly out the window. "Those two look pretty scary to me."

"Burke is a bit of a grump, but he's harmless," said Maru. "Same with Hannibal, his Great Dane."

"What is he doing here?" asked Henry.

Maru sighed. "Probably just checking in. You see, Burke used to own this house. But he had to sell it. It was too much for him to care for anymore."

"That's sad," said Violet.

"There weren't many buyers for an old house with a graveyard next door," said Maru. "But it works well for my business."

"I wonder why no one wanted it," said Jessie. "A house can be fixed, and graveyards are everywhere."

"There were other things too..." said Maru. Her voice trailed off, and Henry wondered what it was she didn't want to tell them.

Just then the back door handle jiggled. "Someone's trying to get in!" Benny cried.

A Visit in the Night

A ghostly white face with deep-set eyes appeared in the window. Maru opened the door and greeted Burke. Hannibal sat behind him, holding a large, white bone in his mouth. His yellow eyes stared at the children.

"Oh, I didn't expect to see you here," Burke said to Maru. He turned to the children, who had gathered at the door. "What are these children doing here?"

Burke had his sleeves rolled up, revealing bony, white arms and long, thin fingers. Benny tried not to stare at the man or his big dog.

"These are friends of ours, Burke," said Maru. "They are helping me decorate for the opening tomorrow. Is there something I can help you with?"

"Oh no, no," stammered Burke. "I'm just, uh, checking to make sure nobody was up to no good." He took a step inside and scowled at the skeleton Violet had placed at the piano. He glared at the strings of lights that Henry and Jessie had put up. He grumbled when he saw the bowls of candy that Benny had set out.

"What do you think of our decorations?" Maru asked.

A Visit in the Night

"It looks like you've turned my home into a tourist trap," said Burke. "I guess we'll see how *that* works for you. Come on, boy."

Without another word, Burke slammed the door and disappeared back into the mist. Hannibal followed close behind, the bone still clutched in his teeth.

"He seemed mad," said Violet.

"And I don't think he liked us being here," said Benny.

"Don't mind Burke," said Maru. "He has a bad history with children."

"Is that what you meant before?" said Henry. "About why no one wanted to buy the house?"

Maru sighed. "I guess I should tell you," she said. "When Burke lived here, people came up with all kinds of stories."

"What kinds of stories?" asked Violet.

"Impossible ones," said Maru. "They said that at night, skeletons in the graveyard came to life, and that Burke was their keeper. The stories described Hannibal as some kind of phantom, roaming the graveyard at night like a ghost."

Benny's eyes got big. "Are the stories true?" he asked.

Maru shook her head. "Of course not," she said. "But that didn't stop people from believing them. Children would dare each other to come up to the house at night and ring the doorbell. Then they would run away. I suppose tonight Burke thought someone might be breaking in. So it was nice of him to check."

For a moment everyone was quiet. Then Henry said, "Should we make sure everything is ready for tomorrow?"

"Yes, let's do that," said Maru. The children followed her back to the escape room. They made sure all the riddles and other clues were in place.

"The riddle about the stars was the hardest one," said Benny.

Henry nodded. "I thought the garden of blossoms was the vase with the flowers."

"It was fun writing those clues," said Maru. "Nick helped. He's very creative that way."

After they were done tidying up, Jessie tucked the key into the pocket of the coffin.

A Visit in the Night

"Why are they called skeleton keys, anyway?" asked Benny. "Do skeletons use them?"

Maru smiled. "Skeleton keys got their name because the top looks like a skull," she said. "They are special keys that can open more than one lock."

Maru saw the worry on Benny's face as they walked back into the lobby. "Don't worry," she said. "I'm the only one with a key to this place."

Just then the front door burst open. A young man with purple-streaked hair entered the room. He was wearing a skull and crossbones T-shirt and black jeans.

"Nick!" said Maru. "Where in the world have you been?"

"I'm so sorry," the young man said. "My band had some last-minute things to do to get ready for the Hammond Hills Town Fair."

Maru frowned. "The festival is not for two days," she said. "I would think that your work here would be more important."

Nick hung his head. "Sorry." He looked around. "It looks like you are about finished decorating and getting things ready for tomorrow."

"Yes, thank goodness the Aldens arrived to help me," said Maru. She introduced the children to Nick.

"I like your hair," said Violet.

"Thanks, Violet," said Nick, smiling. "The decorations look really good," he said. "Did you help with the sign out front? It's very spooky."

"The welcome sign?" asked Maru. "I haven't decorated that yet. It was the last thing to do before tomorrow."

"Well, someone decorated it," said Nick.

Everyone hurried to the front porch to see what Nick was talking about.

"Oh my goodness," said Maru. "It's supposed to say, 'Welcome to the Skeleton Key!'"

Instead, the chalkboard had a drawing of a smirking, white-and-black skull. Underneath, in shaky red letters, were the words, You will NEVER escape!

"That's not a very welcoming sign," said Henry.

"No, it's not," said Maru. "I want to invite people to have fun. Not scare them."

"The sign was blank when we came in," said

A Visit in the Night

Henry. "Someone must have written it while we were inside."

"Someone who wanted to scare people away," said Violet.

Just then Benny heard a noise coming from the cornfield across the dirt road. A tall scarecrow with a wide grin stood at the edge. Behind it, the rows of corn rippled and swayed. Was something moving through the field?

"I like Halloween," Benny said. "But there are lots of spooky things going on around here."

CHAPTER 3

Strangely Similar

"There's a rainbow outside!" Benny said, pointing out the kitchen window. The Aldens, Verónica, and Maru were sitting around a large dining room table. There were bowls of fresh pastries, sliced apples sprinkled with cinnamon, scrambled eggs, and bacon, plus a pitcher of cold milk.

"A rainbow?" asked Jessie. "Benny, it hasn't rained this morning. What are you dreaming up this time?"

"I'm not making it up," said Benny. "Really!"

Jessie peered out the window. Sure enough, up in the sky, the colors of the rainbow shone brightly.

"See? I told you." Benny grinned and reached for a pastry.

"That is a hot-air balloon," said Maru.

"Farmer Dawson sells balloon rides as part of his farm festival," said Verónica. "People go up in the balloon to see all the fall colors from above. They can also get a peek at his giant corn maze below."

"A corn maze?" said Jessie. "We like corn mazes."

"That's right," said Henry. "It's like a memory game where you try and figure out which way you've come and which way you need to go."

"Can we do the corn maze?" Violet asked Grandfather.

"You don't want to go with Verónica and me on our leaf-peeping trip?" Grandfather asked.

"Leaf what?" said Benny.

"Leaf peeping," said Verónica. "It's a funny way of saying, 'looking at the leaves that are changing colors this time of the year.'"

"That sounds *boring*," said Benny. "I want to go to the corn maze!"

Jessie shushed her brother, but she had to admit she wanted to go to the corn maze too.

Grandfather chuckled. "That's okay, Jessie. Why don't you children go and enjoy the corn maze? We can share all of our adventures later today."

"I can drop off the children," said Maru. "The maze is just down the road from the Skeleton Key. They can come and join me when they're done."

Everyone agreed. Once the dishes were done and everyone was ready, the children said good-bye to Grandfather and Verónica and went the opposite way down the country road.

***

The Aldens stood with Maru at the entrance to the corn maze. Waves of cornstalks seemed to stretch forever. There were signs leading to all of the activities at Dawson's Farm Festival, including a pumpkin patch, petting zoo, pig races, and a corn pit.

Violet read the banner hanging over their heads: "'New this year—solve the riddles to win the maze.'"

"Riddles?" said Henry. "That sounds like your escape room, Maru!"

"Interesting," said Maru. "I don't remember there being riddles in the past."

"May I help you?" A deep voice spoke from behind them.

The children turned to find a short man wearing overalls and an orange plaid shirt. He had on a straw hat and wore muddy boots.

"Well, hello there," said Maru. "Children, meet Farmer Dawson. This is his farm."

"Nice to meet you, Farmer Dawson," said Henry. "We would like to go through the corn maze, please."

"We are very good at solving riddles," said Violet.

"We solved a lot of riddles in Maru's escape room!" said Benny.

"You don't say," said Farmer Dawson. "Good for you."

The farmer turned back to Maru. "Speaking of your little business," he continued, "are you about ready to open?"

"Just about, thank you," said Maru. "I've got to run a couple errands this morning. But I will open at noon, just as planned!"

"Well that's just dandy," said Farmer Dawson. "I hope nothing goes wrong."

Violet thought Mr. Dawson had a strange way of wishing Maru luck, but Maru smiled and nodded.

"Thank you," she said. "Now, Aldens, are you ready to try this corn maze?"

"Ready!" the children said at once.

"Okay, I'll see you all later," said Maru. "Good luck!"

Henry paid Farmer Dawson the entry fee as Maru walked back to her cherry-red truck.

"All right," said the farmer. "You have one hour to complete the maze. Be sure to put the clues back where you found them."

Before the children could thank him, Farmer Dawson stalked off.

"He sure seemed like he was in a hurry," said Benny.

"And not too friendly," said Violet.

"I'm sure he's just busy with his festival," said Jessie. "Now, let's get to work!"

Jessie, Violet, and Benny followed Henry into the corn maze. The voices of the other visitors faded until all the children heard was the cornstalks rustling in the breeze. Before long, the trail came to a crossroads with a bale of hay in the center.

"Which way should we go?" said Benny.

"Maybe there's a clue in the hay bale," said Henry.

The children examined the bale, sticking their hands into the straw.

"Oh, I feel something," said Violet. She gently removed an envelope.

"That must be the first riddle," said Jessie. "Let Benny read it!"

Violet took a piece of paper out of the envelope. She handed it to Benny.

"'I have no legs, but I have a head and a tail. Find where I hide, and you'll know where to sail.'"

"Good job, Benny," said Jessie. "Now we have to solve the riddle!" She tucked the clue into the envelope and stuck it back in the hay bale.

"It seems a lot like Maru's escape room," said Violet. "That means the answer will be somewhere in sight."

"That's right," said Henry. "Let's look around."

The children scoured the area around the bale of hay. Before long, Benny lost his patience and plopped down.

"This is a hard clue," he said, swinging his feet

back and forth. Then Benny jumped off the hay bale and squatted down in the dirt. "Hey, it's my lucky day! I found a coin!"

Henry came over to look. "Yes it is, Benny. Because a penny has a head and a tail."

"But no legs!" said Jessie.

"Benny, you solved the riddle!" said Violet.

"I did?" said Benny. "So it means we go this way on the path where I found the penny?"

"I think so," said Henry. "Let's go!"

Benny carefully planted the penny back in the dirt, and the children walked through the maze until they reached a Y in the path. This time there was a scarecrow on a stand in the middle of the path.

"There's a piece of paper hanging from its sleeve," said Jessie. She removed the piece of paper and handed it to Benny. "What does this one tell us?" she asked.

"'A house with no windows, nor doors to behold. Crack me open. Inside, I'm gold,'" Benny read. "What kind of house do you crack open?" he asked. He handed the paper back to Jessie, who clipped it back onto the scarecrow's sleeve.

"Maybe a doll house?" said Violet.

"Or a safe," said Henry. "They don't have windows, and they are full of gold."

"Those are good ideas," said Jessie. "Let's look around."

The children searched, but all they found was the scarecrow.

"This is a hard riddle to solve," said Benny. "I'd rather walk around and try to find the way on my own."

"The only thing I can think of that we crack open is an egg," said Jessie. "I cracked open a lot of them this morning for our breakfast, fresh from the chicken coop."

"But an egg is not a house," said Benny.

"It is for a baby chicken!" said Violet.

"Yes, that must be the answer," said Jessie. "Let's see if we can find an egg."

"Look," said Benny. "There's a nest on the scarecrow's hat!"

"Maybe there is an egg inside," said Henry. He had Benny sit on his shoulders, just like they had done the night before at the escape room. Benny reached in and pulled out a plastic egg from the nest in the scarecrow's hat. He pulled apart the halves, and a plastic letter L dropped to the ground. Violet picked it up.

"What does L mean?" she asked.

"Maybe it's like the arrow from last night," said Jessie. "It's telling us which way to go."

"We can go left or right," said Henry. "That must mean we go to the left." Henry handed the egg back to Benny, who returned it to the nest.

The children riddled their way past spooky ghouls and a gruesome mummy. They even made their way through a giant spiderweb.

"This is a creepy maze!" said Violet. "I'm glad there are the four of us!"

"It reminds me more and more of the Skeleton Key," said Jessie.

"Yes it does," agreed Henry. "And the riddles are a new part of the maze this year. Isn't it strange that Farmer Dawson started doing that at the same time Maru opened her escape room?"

When the children arrived at the end of the maze, a grinning skeleton suddenly dropped down from the exit sign, jiggling its bones.

"Ah!" cried Benny. "A living skeleton!"

"It's not," Jessie assured her little brother. "It's just another fun prop for the maze."

Benny watched the skeleton move in the breeze, its dry bones rattling. He looked at the smirk on its face. It looked like more than just another fun prop to him. It reminded him of the creepy skull they had found on the welcome sign the night before.

"You made it in less than one hour," said Farmer Dawson, waiting at the exit. "I guess you win." He handed them a ticket. "You can use this to pay for your pumpkin."

"Thank you!" said Violet. "Where are the pumpkins?"

"Just follow the signs to the pumpkin patch," said Farmer Dawson. "I'll meet you over there in a few minutes."

The children walked to the pumpkin patch and picked out their free pumpkin. They waited for Farmer Dawson so they could give him the ticket.

"Look, it's the rainbow balloon!" said Violet. She pointed up at the hot-air balloon as it slowly lowered to the ground in an open part of the field. A crew of people surrounded it as it landed.

"It's beautiful," said Jessie. "Just like a rainbow, like Benny said. I wonder how much it costs to go for a ride."

"I could take some pretty photos from up there," said Violet.

"There's a sign here," said Henry. "Oh my. It's very expensive."

"But it says here you can win a free ride," said Jessie.

"How?" Benny asked. He looked at the sign. There were too many words for him to read.

"It says the winner of the jack-o'-lantern carving competition at the Hammond Hills Town Fair will get a free ride for four people," said Jessie.

"Oh!" cried Violet. "We can carve our pumpkin and enter it in the contest!"

"And win a free balloon ride!" said Benny.

"Let's buy three more pumpkins so we each can enter," said Henry. "That will give us a better chance of winning."

"Good idea," said Benny. "I have a perfect idea

for a spooky jack-o'-lantern."

The children found three more pumpkins to go with their prize.

"These pumpkins are expensive too," said Henry. "It's a good thing that we got the first one for free."

"Who do we pay?" asked Jessie. "Farmer Dawson said he'd be here in a few minutes. But that was a long time ago."

"I don't see him anywhere," said Violet. "Maybe he forgot."

As the children waited to pay for their pumpkins, they watched the hot-air balloon crew tie it down. "Maybe the pilot can take our money for the pumpkins," said Henry.

They strode across the field to the balloon. A young woman greeted them. She was wearing jeans and a black T-shirt with a skull and crossbones on it.

"Hi, I'm Zoey," she said.

"Hi, Zoey," said Violet. "You have on the same tee shirt as Nick, Maru's helper."

"Cool," said Zoey. "You can pay me for those

pumpkins, please."

"We thought Farmer Dawson would be here," said Jessie, handing her the money.

"Dad had to run an errand," said Zoey. "He texted me that you would be at the pumpkin patch."

"That's funny," said Benny. "Maru is also doing errands. She's getting things ready for her escape room."

"What else could she possibly need?" asked Zoey. "It's all set up and decorated, ready to open this afternoon."

Jessie thought it was odd that Zoey seemed to know all about the Skeleton Key, since it hadn't opened yet. "Just some last-minute things," she said.

"Whatever," said Zoey. "Here's your change. I have to get back to work now." Zoey handed the coins to Jessie and marched back to the hot-air balloon.

"Let's go see how things are going at the Skeleton Key," said Henry, looking at his watch. "It opened just a little while ago."

The children took the short walk down the road

to the Skeleton Key. As they approached, Benny looked at the scarecrow that had glowed the night before. In the light of day, it didn't seem nearly as spooky. Benny was starting to think that Jessie was right. Maybe he had been letting his imagination get the best of him.

Just then, a scream came from inside the Skeleton Key.

CHAPTER

4

A Not-So-Grand Opening

The Aldens ran up to the porch just as a family of four was storming out. A man and a woman and two young children scrambled down the stairs.

"This was supposed to be a fun adventure!" the man said. "Not a house of horrors!"

"We were frightened out of our wits! The kids are very upset," said the woman.

"That skeleton tried to grab me!" cried one of the children.

"Then there was a message...it looked like it was written in blood!" cried the other. The family raced toward Dawson's Farm Festival.

"It sounds like something terrible happened," said Henry.

"Let's go find Maru," said Jessie. The children raced inside.

Maru was in the escape room with Nick. The Aldens stared into the room in wonder. Maru looked very upset.

"What happened in here, Nick?" she asked. "Everything was set up last evening!"

"I don't know," said Nick. "I didn't have time to check it before you let those people inside."

The room was completely different from how it was the night before. The skull clock had pumpkin guts oozing out of the mouth. The vase of flowers was shattered, and the flowers were scattered on the floor. Inside the coffin, the skeleton decoration Violet had placed on the piano bench was standing upright.

Benny reached for Jessie's hand. "How...how did the skeleton get there?"

"Oh! Look at the mirror," said Violet. On the large, dusty mirror, someone had drawn a shaky-looking skeleton.

"It's just like the skeleton on the welcome sign last night!" said Henry.

At the top of the mirror, someone had written a message in red letters. "'You will never escape!'" read Benny. The spooky words made him reach for Jessie's hand.

"That's exactly what was written on the welcome sign," said Violet.

"At first the family figured it was just part of the puzzle," said Maru.

"What happened to scare them so much?" asked Henry. "Was it the skeleton in the coffin?"

Maru shook her head. "They said they heard a scratching noise on the window," she said. "It sounded to them like fingertips on the glass."

"Yikes," said Violet. "That would sure scare me!"

"It *did* scare them," said Maru. "They banged on the door to be released. I opened the door, and they ran out. I still haven't found the key."

"Wow, scratching on the window—that's a nice touch," said Nick. "I wish I'd thought of it!"

Maru scowled at her employee. "None of these things were supposed to be part of my escape room. The purpose is to have fun, not to scare people!"

Nick hung his head. "I just wanted to cheer you

up," he said. "I guess I should set the room back to how it should be?"

"Yes, please do that," said Maru. "And I will help you make sure it's done right."

The Aldens left Maru and Nick to tidy up, while they searched for clues.

"It looks like what happened to those customers really scared people," said Henry. "I don't see anyone else coming to try the escape room."

"I wouldn't want to be trapped in a room haunted by a skeleton either," said Benny.

"Oh, Benny," said Jessie. "That's just your imagination talking again."

The Aldens scanned the lobby to see if anything else was out of place. Then Violet heard a noise coming from the back of the house.

"Did anyone else hear that?" she asked. The children were quiet as they listened.

The sound was soft but clear. *Scritch, scratch. Scritch, scratch.*

"See?" Benny whispered. "I told you. It's that sound that scared away those people!"

Jessie knew that there was no such thing as

living skeletons, but even she had to admit the noise sounded like a bony finger scratching across glass.

"It's coming from out back," said Henry. "By the graveyard."

Jessie took a deep breath. "There must be an explanation," she said. "Let's go and look."

She led the way to the back door and turned the handle. Quietly, the children headed outside. Benny stayed close to Henry.

"I don't hear the noise," said Jessie. "Let's go check the window outside the escape room. Maybe a tree branch was making that sound."

The children crept along behind the house and peeked around the corner. To Benny's relief, there was nothing by the window.

"No branches," said Jessie. "I wonder where that noise was coming from."

"Maybe mice were scratching on the window," said Violet.

"That's a good idea, Violet," said Henry. "But I don't think a mouse could climb up to the window."

"Are there any footprints?" asked Jessie. She

looked around the leaf-covered ground in front of the window.

"There won't be footprints in the dry leaves," said Henry. "But look! There are scratches in the paint on the window."

"Someone was definitely here," said Violet.

Scritch, scratch. Scritch, scratch.

This time, it was clear the noise was coming from the backyard. The Aldens made their way back around the corner of the house.

Scritch, scratch. Scritch, scratch.

Beyond the gate, they found the source of the sound. Burke was in the graveyard, raking leaves. The children walked up to him.

"What do you kids want?" he asked.

"We heard scratching noises," said Henry. "We were wondering where they came from."

"Well, I'm raking leaves," said Burke, holding his rake out toward them. "Is that a problem for you?"

Violet noticed the rake shook as Burke held it. Could the shaky handwriting on the chalkboard have been from him?

"We think somebody was trying to scare people

away from the Skeleton Key," said Jessie. "Did you see anyone back here?"

"What happens in that tourist trap is no longer my concern," Burke replied. "I warned Maru that the old house came with problems. They are her problems now."

Henry noticed that Burke had not answered the question. But without another word, the old man turned and headed away into the graveyard, grumbling.

"Let's go back into the house," said Henry. "Maybe we can find more clues about what happened there."

As the children walked back to the house, Violet paused to take a picture. The night before, the graveyard had looked scary. But now there was something beautiful about the well-kept grounds and the large trees in their fall colors.

When she was done taking pictures, Violet turned back to the house. In the grass next to the door, she noticed something shiny and picked it up. It was long and thin and made of metal. The object reminded her of the tools she used in art class to carve shapes into clay. What was it doing outside?

The wind blew and gave Violet a chill. Without thinking twice, she slipped the object into her workbag and went inside.

***

The children explored the living room. They looked inside the piano and behind the furniture. They investigated the light strings and the fake spiderwebs. Besides the skeleton moving from the piano to the escape room, everything was just as they'd left it, even the bowls of candy. Then Violet checked the desk by the front door.

"Look!" she cried. She held up the skeleton key. "It was underneath a pile of papers on the desk!"

"Wow," said Jessie. "That means that poor family really was locked inside the escape room!"

"That's scary," said Benny. "No wonder they were so upset."

Maru and Nick appeared.

"Everything is back together now," said Maru. "But the key is still missing."

Violet handed the key to Maru. "We found it

under a pile of papers on the desk," she said.

Maru stared at the key and then handed it to Nick. "Put this in its place, please," she said. "Then you may go back to your band practice."

Nick replaced the key and left the house, not saying a word. Maru sat down at the desk and stared out the window.

"It looks like nobody else is coming to my grand opening," she said with a sigh.

"Are you closing the Skeleton Key?" asked Violet.

"I think I will close for now," said Maru. "I'm tired. I will open again tomorrow for the town fair."

"Who would do something like this?" asked Jessie. "Do you have any idea?"

"I sure don't," said Maru. "I am shocked that someone seems to want to hurt my new business."

When Maru said these words, wind rattled the little window inside the escape room.

"Did you find any clues outside?" she asked.

"We found scratches on the window," said Henry. "Someone had been there, all right."

"Burke was raking leaves," said Jessie. "But he didn't seem to want to talk to us."

A Not-So-Grand Opening

Maru sighed again and sat down at the reception desk. "Maybe Burke was right to sell this place. Maybe it's more trouble than it's worth."

"You said Nick was here when you got to the house this morning?" Henry asked.

"No," said Maru. "Nick showed up after I arrived. He was late, as usual."

"Could he have changed things when you were out running errands?" said Jessie.

"He did seem pretty uncaring about how bad the opening went," said Violet.

"And he thought that creepy scratching was a good idea!" added Benny.

Maru shook her head. "Nick isn't the most reliable employee, but I don't think he would do something like that."

"That means someone must have changed things before you got here," said Henry.

"How could someone have gotten in?" said Maru. "I know I locked up before we left last night. And I have the only key."

"Maybe someone does have a key," said Benny. "A key that can open any lock—a skeleton key!"

"Oh, Benny," said Jessie. "You and your imagination!" But Jessie had to admit that even she did not have a better explanation for what was going on.

CHAPTER 5

Carving and a Clue

"We should carve our pumpkins after we're done," said Violet. The children were back at Verónica's house and had just finished a late lunch.

"Good idea!" said Henry. He handed a clean plate to Benny, who dried it with a towel and handed it to Jessie.

"We'll need to spread out newspapers for the mess," said Jessie, putting the plate into the cupboard.

"We'll need carving tools too," said Violet.

"There's a stack of newspapers by the window," said Maru. "I'll bring in the pumpkin-carving tools from the shed. Then I think I'm going to take a nap. It's been a long day."

Maru headed outside, letting the screen door slap behind her.

"Maru looks tired and discouraged," Violet said as she gathered up newspapers.

"Yes, she does," said Jessie. "And unhappy."

"I would be unhappy too," said Benny, "if a skeleton was haunting my house!"

Henry ignored his little brother's mention of skeletons. "It definitely wasn't a very grand opening," he said sadly.

The children worked together to spread newspapers over the dining room table and floor.

"We can save all the scraps for Verónica's chickens," said Benny. "They love pumpkin seeds!"

Maru came back inside and gave Henry a box. "Everything you'll need is in here," she said. "Mom saved her collection of carving tools from when she was a teacher."

"Thank you," said Violet. "We'll have fun carving pumpkins for the contest tomorrow!"

"Okay," said Maru. "I really do need a nap. We can go to Tilly Gorts restaurant for dinner later. So don't worry about messing up the kitchen!"

"Rest well," said Jessie. "We will clean up."

"Thank you, Jessie," said Maru. She headed to her room.

They pulled out tools from the box.

"We just *have* to figure out who ruined Maru's escape room," said Violet, carving a hole in the top of her pumpkin. "I feel so bad for her."

"The first question we need to answer is why someone would want to hurt her business," said Henry.

"Good point, Henry," said Jessie. "I think Burke is a suspect. He could be mad that she bought his house and turned it into a business."

Violet nodded. "He said that the house's problems were Maru's problems now. What do you think he meant by that?"

"I think he meant that the living skeletons from the graveyard are her problem now," Benny said.

"Those are just made-up stories, Benny," said Jessie. "There must be a better explanation."

"I think Nick is a suspect," said Henry. "He doesn't seem interested in doing his job."

"And he likes scary things," added Benny.

"He doesn't have a key," said Jessie. "But he could have left himself a way in and come back later in the night."

"I don't know," Violet said. "He seems nice. And he's very creative too. Maru said he helped a lot with the Skeleton Key."

"You're right," said Jessie. "It's hard to imagine Nick wanting to do something mean to a project that he was a big part of."

"Well, someone creative messed with the welcome sign," said Henry.

"What about Farmer Dawson?" asked Jessie.

"His corn maze was a lot like Maru's secret room, wasn't it?" said Henry. "And he wasn't all that friendly to Maru this morning either."

"All three of them are suspects," said Jessie. "But we still don't have much evidence."

For a while, the children worked quietly on their pumpkins. Henry's jack-o'-lantern had a goofy, gap-toothed grin. Jessie's was a cat with long whiskers and a waving paw. Benny made a drooping skeleton on his tall, skinny pumpkin.

Violet had something different in mind for her

carving. But she needed just the right tool to add the finishing touches, and none of the tools in the box were quite right. Then she remembered the metal object she found in the grass behind the Skeleton Key. It had a fine, sharp tip that would be perfect!

When she was done, Violet turned the pumpkin to her brothers and sister.

"Wow!" said Jessie. "That's very creative, Violet."

"That will win for sure!" said Benny.

"How did you get such small details?" asked Henry.

Violet told them about the tool she had found behind the Skeleton Key.

Henry looked over the strange tool. "I think this might be helpful in two ways," he said.

"Two ways?" asked Jessie. "What do you mean?"

"I mean that it might help Violet win the pumpkin-carving competition," said Henry. "And I have a feeling it might be the key to solving our mystery."

Just then Grandfather and Verónica walked in.

"Wow, it looks like a pumpkin-carving factory in here," said Verónica. "I see Maru found my carving tools."

"We won a free pumpkin in the corn maze today," said Benny.

"We bought the others," said Violet. "We want to win the pumpkin-carving contest tomorrow so we can get a free ride in the hot-air balloon."

"It sounds like you had fun today," said Grandfather.

"Well, it wasn't all fun..." said Jessie.

"Somebody sabotaged Maru's Skeleton Key escape room," Henry explained.

"That's terrible," said Grandfather. "Does Maru know who did it?"

"Not yet," said Henry.

"But we are all working on it!" said Benny.

"Well, as always, you children have found yourselves a mystery to solve," said Grandfather. "But you missed a beautiful day to be out looking at the leaves."

"It was gorgeous," agreed Verónica. "We walked a lot!" She sat at the table and pulled off her shoes.

"It's still a beautiful day," said Jessie. "We could go look at the leaves around here."

"Maru said we can go to a restaurant in town for dinner later," said Henry.

"She's taking a nap," said Benny. "She was very tired."

"I'm not surprised," said Verónica. "I'll go and check on her."

"And I'll sit in that comfortable chair over there and read my book," said Grandfather. "Have fun!"

The children gathered up the newspapers and placed their pumpkins back on the dining room table. Then they put on their coats and took the newspapers out to the chicken yard.

"Here you go, chickens!" said Benny. He tossed seeds and pulp to the chickens. The others joined in.

"Those are happy chickens," said Benny. "I hope they give us more eggs for breakfast tomorrow!"

The children found a path leading into the colorful woods.

"This path goes along to the road," said Jessie. "That means we'll be heading toward the Skeleton Key."

"Good," said Violet. "We won't get lost!" She snapped photos of yellow beech trees, red sumac, and fiery red and yellow sugar maples.

"Why do tree leaves change their colors in the fall?" she asked.

"The leaves don't exactly change," said Henry. "They just lose their green."

"Huh?" asked Benny.

"In fall, the trees stop letting water get to their

leaves," said Henry. "That makes their chlorophyll—the stuff that makes leaves green—go away. Without the green, the other leaf colors appear."

"But why do the trees do that?" Violet asked.

"The trees are getting ready to sleep all winter," said Henry.

"That's a fun idea," said Benny. "I'd like to sleep all winter too!"

The children walked along the path, admiring the foliage. Soon they came to the edge of an old graveyard. It was surrounded by a wooden fence.

"Is...is this the graveyard behind the Skeleton Key?" asked Benny.

"I guess so," said Henry. "It's much bigger than I thought."

"The gravestones here look even older," said Jessie. "They look ancient."

The children walked along the fence, admiring the stones and wondering about the people buried there so long ago. They came to an open gate.

"That's strange," said Violet. "I'm sure Burke doesn't want people coming in through this entrance."

"Or his dog, Hannibal, getting out," said Jessie. "Maybe we should close it for him."

"That looks like Burke's toolshed," said Henry. He pointed to a place where the gravestones ended and a small shed stood. "Let's see if he's there."

"Maybe we should just close the gate and go back," said Benny. The sun was setting, and under the tall, old trees, it was starting to get dark.

"It will only take a second, Benny," said Henry, leading the way through the gate. "We don't want Hannibal getting out and getting lost. Imagine if that happened to Watch."

As they got closer, Henry thought he heard a scratching sound coming from around the shed. But when they turned the corner, no one was there.

"That's strange," said Henry. "I thought for sure I heard something. Oh well. Maybe Benny's right, and we should head back."

But something had already caught Benny's eye. "Wha...what's that?" he asked.

The children looked to where Benny was pointing. In front of the toolshed was a shallow hole in the ground. The Aldens walked over and peered inside.

"It's a skeleton!" cried Benny, hiding behind Jessie.

Jessie looked closer. Sure enough, at the bottom of the hole sat a pile of bleach-white bones.

"Why would there be bones here?" asked Violet. "It's not a grave."

Henry examined the hole. "There are scratch marks all around it," he said. "An animal probably did this."

Benny thought back to the stories of the skeletons coming alive at night, and of Hannibal, the big phantom dog. He looked around at the shadows creeping out from the old woods. "I think we should go back to the house," he said.

"Good idea," said Jessie. "We'll figure out what's going on when the sun is out again."

The children hurried out of the graveyard, closing the gate behind them.

CHAPTER 6

A Warning

"We didn't bring any costumes with us," Violet said the next morning, looking sadly at the clothes in her suitcase. It was the day of the town fair, and she wanted to wear something special.

"Maybe we can make our costumes," said Jessie.

"Let's see if Verónica has any old clothes," said Henry.

Verónica and Maru were in the kitchen with Grandfather, finishing their coffee.

"Look up in the attic," said Verónica. "I do have some old costumes and clothes stored. I'm sure you can cobble something together."

"I'm sure they will," said Grandfather. "Thank you, Verónica."

A Warning

"I wish I could come with you all, but I've got to be at the Skeleton Key," said Maru.

"We hope things go better today," said Henry.

"I do too," said Maru. "Please apologize to Nick when you see him. I will miss his band's performance at the town fair."

"We will," said Jessie. "Good luck!"

The children headed up to the attic to search for costumes. Henry found a pirate costume that fit. Jessie found a stethoscope and hung it around her neck. She put on a white jacket.

"Just call me Doctor Alden," she said, smiling.

Violet found a purple butterfly costume.

"There's nothing here that fits me," said Benny.

"We'll make you something," said Jessie. "What would you like to be?"

"That's okay," said Benny. "I just got an idea. You'll see my costume later!"

***

"Wow, it sure looks different from last night's dinner at Tilly Gorts," said Jessie. The children had taken the short walk from Verónica's house to the town fair. The street was closed to cars, and people were walking in all directions, visiting the many displays and booths.

"And what are you dressed up to be, young man?" asked a woman passing by the children.

Benny was wearing his orange sweatshirt and black jeans. He had on a red baseball cap with tree leaves pinned to it and the sweatshirt.

"I am a tree getting ready to sleep all winter!" said Benny.

"Very clever," chuckled the woman. "Have a fun day!"

"Thank you," said Benny. "You too!"

There were carnival games, a farmers market, and all kinds of displays surrounding the town square. In the middle, a stage had been set up. All of the stores up and down the street were covered with festive decorations.

Henry found a map of the fair at the welcome booth.

"Let's go and enter our pumpkins in the jack-o'-lantern competition," said Henry. "Then we can see what else is happening."

Henry led the way to the competition area.

A Warning

Cleverly carved pumpkins were placed all around on tables.

"These jack-o'-lanterns are wonderful," said Jessie. "We have a lot of competition."

"It will be fun to see which one wins," said Violet.

The judging would happen later on, so the Aldens wandered through the fair. There were crafts, food booths, and lots of games to play.

Benny pointed at a sign over a water trough. "Bob for apples! Are you Bob?" he asked.

"My name is Jeff," said a boy standing by the trough, smiling. "It costs ten cents to bob for an apple."

"What does bob for apples mean?" asked Benny.

"It means you grab an apple out of the water with your teeth," explained Jeff.

"And using no hands!" said Jessie.

"I can do that," said Benny. "I'm good at getting food in my mouth." He handed his hat to Jessie, put his hands behind his back, and tried to catch an apple in the trough. He went for the biggest apple first, but as soon as he touched it, the apple sank below the water. Benny tried to grab a smaller one, but it disappeared even more quickly. He gasped for air. "They're slippery!" he said.

"Push one into the side of the trough using your chin," said Violet.

Benny nudged the biggest apple to the back of the trough. Pinning it up against the wall, he was able to sink his teeth into it. Benny yanked up his head with the apple in his mouth.

The Aldens cheered.

Jessie gave him back his leaf-colored hat. "Now you're an apple tree!" she said with a laugh.

"That was fun," said Benny. He shared his apple with the other children.

"I wonder how Maru is doing today," said Violet.

"She looked very worried," said Jessie. "I hope nothing bad happens at the Skeleton Key again."

"I wish we knew what was going on there," said Henry. "I hate to think someone was really trying to hurt her business."

"Well, maybe right now we should have some fun," said Jessie.

"We might get a new idea while we are here," said Violet. "Ideas are like that sometimes."

"That's true," said Henry.

"What will we do now?" asked Benny.

"That looks like fun," said Violet. She pointed to a booth nearby.

"Face painting!" said Benny. "Let's do it."

"I'm game," said Jessie.

"I'll watch the rest of you," said Henry.

Violet, Benny, and Jessie giggled as they let the artist paint their faces. Violet got a butterfly on her cheek. The artist painted autumn leaves on Benny's cheek. Jessie decided she wanted four hearts.

"One heart for each of us," she said.

Henry snapped a picture with Violet's camera. "You all look terrific," he said. "What's next?"

"Let's go look at all the Halloween decorations," said Violet.

"Good idea," said Jessie. "We can come back later and see if any of our pumpkins won the jack-o'-lantern contest."

They walked around town and admired the holiday decorations. The whole town looked like it was celebrating. Giant balloon figures floated above them, each streetlamp had a scarecrow attached, and costumed characters roamed the sidewalks.

"Look at all the ghosts and ghouls walking around," said Violet. "Some of them are a little creepy!"

"It's all in good fun," said Jessie. She waved at a ghoul that passed them, and the ghoul waved back.

A post-office worker dressed as a pony express rider was handing out free movie passes to passersby. Outside the bank, two people were dressed up as bank robbers. A tall man stood by while a shorter man tried to open a safe on the sidewalk.

"What's in there?" asked Benny.

"You'll see very soon," the tall man said in a friendly voice.

"Are you going to get it open?" asked Violet.

The shorter man turned and said, "All doors can be opened with the right tools."

With that, the door to the safe sprang open. The fake robbers tossed bags of candy to the crowd.

"A candy vault!" said Benny, digging in to grab some chocolate.

While her siblings shared the candy, Violet was thinking about what the man had said. If any door could be opened with the right tools, could someone have used tools to get into Maru's old house?

"Oh, look, isn't that Burke and Hannibal?" said Henry. He pointed to a stooped figure and a large black dog walking a little ways down the street. The dog's eyes gleamed yellow against its pitch-black face.

"It is," said Benny. "Let's wait here, please." With the town fair, Benny had almost forgotten about what they had seen in the graveyard the night before. He stood close to the others as Burke and Hannibal went inside a pet store.

"What does a phantom dog need from a pet store?" asked Benny.

"Who knows?" laughed Jessie. "Phantom dogs don't eat pet food. Maybe Burke is buying him special phantom food!"

Still, Jessie could tell her little brother was getting worried. "Why don't we head back to the fair and check on our jack-o'-lanterns?" she said, taking Benny's hand.

"Good idea," said Henry, looking at his watch. "It's almost time for Nick's band to play!"

A Warning

The Aldens walked back to the town fair and headed to the jack-o'-lantern competition. The pumpkins were set up under a big tent, and a candle had been placed in each one. All around, silly, happy, angry, and spooky faces glowed. One pumpkin was set up on a stand above the others. It didn't have a face at all. Instead, a beautiful array of leaves were carved into its sides, glowing red and orange and yellow. Next to the pumpkin sat a big blue ribbon.

"Violet," said Jessie. "That's your pumpkin! You won first prize!"

"Congratulations!" the fair volunteer said. "What a perfect pumpkin for Hammond Hills."

Violet blushed as the volunteer gave her four tickets for the hot-air balloon at Dawson's Farm.

"Listen," said Jessie. "The band sounds like it's about to start playing. Let's go see the concert."

In a few minutes, Nick took center stage. He had an electric guitar strapped to his chest. He grinned at the Aldens, who had managed to find front-row seats.

As Nick started playing, his guitar sounded

like something from a spooky movie. Then the organist added low, eerie chords. The bass player and drummer followed with a deep rhythm.

"They're really good," said Henry. "Very professional!"

Just then a cloaked figure with a skeleton face burst from behind a black curtain at the back of the stage.

"That's Zoey, from the corn maze!" said Violet. "I recognize her, even with the cape and the scary makeup."

"That's strange," said Jessie. "Nick didn't mention she was in his band."

"And Zoey didn't say anything either," whispered Henry. "Even when Violet noticed she had on the same tee shirt as Nick."

Zoey sang haunting lyrics as the band played on. The crowd cheered after each spooky song. The Aldens cheered along with them.

But as the musicians took their final bow, something happened to make the crowd's cheers go quiet. A banner unfurled from the back of the stage, showing a smirking, black-and-white skeleton. Below it, in red letters, were the words, YOU WILL NEVER ESCAPE!

"Wow!" said Henry. "Look at that!"

Some people in the crowd started to laugh, thinking it was just another Halloween joke. Others weren't so sure.

"That's the same message from that horrible escape room!" someone said. It was the woman who had stormed out of the Skeleton Key with her family the day before. "We were trapped inside!"

"I heard about that," someone said. "There is definitely something wrong with that house."

"It should be torn down, if you ask me," said another person.

As the crowd slowly went their separate ways, the Alden children waited to talk to Nick. They had promised to send good wishes from Maru. And now they had some questions for him too.

CHAPTER

7

Up, Up, and Away!

Nick greeted the Aldens next to the stage. The other band members were packing up their equipment and loading it into a van. Zoey was nowhere to be seen.

"That was a great concert," said Jessie.

"We all thought it was really good," said Henry.

"Thank you," said Nick. "I'm glad you could come."

"The music was a little creepy!" said Violet.

"Only a little?" Nick laughed. "We need to do better next time!"

"Where did Zoey go?" asked Benny.

"She had to get back to the farm to take care of the hot-air balloon," said Nick. "And I need to go to the Skeleton Key to give Maru a break."

"The farm festival is just across the road," said Jessie. "Maybe we can ride along with you?"

"My jack-o'-lantern won four tickets for the rainbow balloon," said Violet.

"Congratulations!" said Nick. "Sure, you can have a ride. Let's go."

Nick had to maneuver the van around booths, tents, and other cars to reach the main road. Soon they were on their way.

"That big banner at the end—was that part of your act?" asked Henry.

"Oh, that? No, it wasn't," said Nick. "But it was a nice way to end our concert, wasn't it?" He smiled.

Violet noticed that Nick seemed to like things to be as scary as possible. "But the banner frightened people," she said. "A lot of them thought it had something to do with what happened at the Skeleton Key."

"I don't know why someone would have it in for the Skeleton Key," said Nick. "But still, it could turn out to be good advertising, don't you think?"

"We're not so sure about that," said Henry. "The

people we overheard wanted the house to be torn down."

"Gosh, I hope it doesn't come to that," said Nick. "Do you believe the rumors? About the skeletons?"

Benny was about to speak up, but Jessie spoke first.

"There's no such thing as living skeletons or haunted houses," she said. "There is an explanation for what's going on. We just don't have it yet."

Nick drove along in silence until they arrived at Dawson's Farm.

"Here's your stop," he said. "Enjoy your balloon ride!"

"Thanks," said Jessie.

"Say hello to Maru, please," said Benny.

"I will do that, Benny," said Nick. "See you all later!"

The Aldens walked around the edge of the corn maze and headed toward the open field where the balloon was anchored. On the way, they noticed Farmer Dawson next to the maze exit. He was loading something into the back of his truck.

"Hi, Farmer Dawson," said Benny. "Isn't that the skeleton from the end of the maze?"

Farmer Dawson seemed startled to see the children.

"Oh, this? Yes, it is. I'm closing the corn maze for the day." He scowled at the children. "Where are you off to, anyway?"

"Violet's jack-o'-lantern won first prize at the town fair competition," said Henry.

"The prize was four tickets to ride in the rainbow balloon," said Violet.

"Isn't that swell?" said Farmer Dawson. He struggled with the skeleton, finally letting it drop with a clatter into the back of the truck. The skeleton knocked over a can, sending nails rolling under a pile of tree branches. Farmer Dawson grumbled and climbed into his truck. The children offered to help, but the man just waved them away.

"What a grump," said Benny. "Let's get going before the balloon ride closes."

"Why was he loading the maze skeleton into his truck?" asked Jessie. "He'll just have to bring it back tomorrow."

"That does seem strange," said Henry.

"Maybe he's afraid the skeleton will run away," said Benny.

"You and your skeletons," said Henry, laughing. "Look, I see Zoey up ahead. Let's get there before she closes down for the day!"

The children hurried to where Zoey stood, leaning on the hot-air balloon basket and texting on her phone. She put her phone away when the Aldens approached.

"Hey, what's up?" she asked. "We were about to close."

Zoey had changed out of her stage costume. Violet noticed only a little bit of the scary makeup on her face.

"Are we too late for our free hot-air balloon ride?" Violet asked. She showed Zoey the four winning tickets.

"Um, I guess not," said Zoey. "I was planning on going up one more time today anyway. Get in!"

"Thank you," said Jessie. She wondered why Zoey would want to take the balloon up with no customers.

Up, Up, and Away!

The Aldens piled into the big wicker basket. Zoey worked some controls, and flames appeared over their heads.

"Oh my goodness!" said Violet. "Why is there a fire?"

"The balloon needs hot air to rise," said Henry. "Don't worry, the balloon is fireproof."

"That's right," said Zoey. "The balloon traps the hot air that those burners make." She waved at a crew member and said, "Let her go!"

The crew member untied the ropes, and the balloon slowly lifted into the air.

"But how do we get back down?" asked Benny. He peered down at the landscape getting smaller and smaller.

"I just pull this cord," said Zoey. "It controls a vent on the top. When the vent opens, the hot air escapes, and we slowly go down to the ground."

"That's a relief," said Violet.

As the balloon rose, Zoey pulled out her phone and started texting again. The children perched on the other side of the wicker basket and watched the scenery below. With the sun just beginning to set, it was the perfect time to go up in the balloon. For a little while, the children were quiet as they drifted higher and higher.

"Everything seems so far away when we're on the ground," Violet said. "But up here, you can see it all at once."

"The people look like little ants!" said Benny.

"Look, there's the Skeleton Key," said Henry. "Nick just pulled up to the front."

"And there goes Maru," said Jessie. She pointed at the cherry-red pickup truck heading away. "She's probably tired from working all day by herself."

Violet noticed that Zoey was still busy texting on her phone and not paying attention to the balloon. "I hope customers came to the Skeleton Key today," Violet said.

This seemed to catch Zoey's ear. She finally put her phone back into her pocket. Zoey fiddled with the controls and looked out over the scenery.

"I just love it up here," she said, changing the subject. "You can see the town fair over that way." She pointed in the other direction.

Henry noticed how Zoey seemed to avoid the

subject of the Skeleton Key. "We sure enjoyed your dad's corn maze yesterday," he said.

"We liked the riddles as clues to solve the maze," said Jessie. "The sign on the corn maze said that part was new this year."

"I solved the penny clue!" said Benny.

Violet picked up on what her older brother and sister were getting at. "The puzzles reminded us of the riddles at the Skeleton Key," she said.

The children looked at Zoey.

"My dad's corn maze has been in business for a very long time," said Zoey, scowling. "He came up with something new this year. So what?"

"I guess people can come up with the same ideas at the same time," said Jessie.

"It just seems like a big coincidence," said Violet.

"Whatever," said Zoey. "The corn maze has been a successful business year after year. A stupid escape room opening up close by doesn't bother us at all."

For a little while, no one spoke. Jessie was surprised at how defensive Zoey seemed to get. She looked down at the corn maze and noticed Farmer

Up, Up, and Away!

Dawson's truck heading out of the farm.

"Look at the colors over to the west, where the sun is setting," said Zoey. "This has been one of our most colorful autumns ever."

The balloon floated along on a gentle breeze, revealing a landscape painted in bright colors. The Aldens admired the colorful rolling hills and golden fields. After a little while, Zoey stood up and adjusted the controls.

"That's the end of the ride," she said. "Let's bring her down." She pulled the vent cord and carefully let the balloon descend. It drifted down on the far side of the field near the corn maze. Near the ground, Zoey threw a line to a crew member, who began tying it off.

"I hope you enjoyed your prize-winning ride," she said.

"It was lots of fun!" said Benny.

"Yes it was," said Jessie. "Thank you very much for your tour of the beautiful landscape."

"No problem," said Zoey. She helped the crew anchor the balloon, turning her back on the children.

The Skeleton Key Mystery

"Let's go over to the Skeleton Key," said Henry. "Maybe Maru is back from her break by now."

The children walked down the road. As they approached, they saw Maru's cherry-red pickup parked outside the Skeleton Key. Nick's car was parked in front of it.

This time, no one was running out of the old house screaming. Instead, Maru was sitting on the porch with her head down, staring at the porch floor.

Close to the Bone

The children surrounded Maru on the porch.

"Are you okay?" asked Henry.

"I'm fine, thanks," said Maru. "But my business isn't. I'm ruined."

Jessie looked inside the window and saw Nick sitting at the desk, wearing headphones.

"Did you have any customers?" she asked.

"Oh yes," said Maru. "I had several customers this morning. Everything was going great."

"Did something happen while you took a break?" asked Henry.

"Yes. Nick had a big group. He said they'd just heard that the Skeleton Key was haunted but wanted to try it anyway."

They must have heard about the banner at the concert, Henry thought.

"What happened to the group?" asked Violet.

"While they were in the escape room, they heard that scratching sound," said Maru. "You know, the one from yesterday? The group didn't think anything of it at first. Then they got really scared."

"Why?" asked Benny. "Was it a skeleton?"

"I don't know what to think," said Maru. "They said they heard the sound of marching bones—an army of them."

"Marching bones?" asked Violet. "What does that sound like?"

Maru shook her head. "I don't know. But it scared the wits out of them."

"Did Nick hear anything?" said Henry.

"I haven't spoken to him," said Maru. "I got here just as the group was running out. They told me what happened and promised to tell others not to come."

"Let's talk to Nick," said Jessie.

"Do you want me to stay out here with you?" asked Violet.

"That's sweet of you, Violet," said Maru. "But I'll be okay. I'm just going to sit and think about what happens next."

Violet followed her siblings into the house. Nick was tapping his fingers and staring at the desk. It didn't seem like he knew they were there.

"Nick?" Henry rapped on the desk. Nick looked up and took off his headphones.

"Oh, hi," he said. "Did Maru tell you what happened?"

"Yes, she did," said Jessie. "Did you see or hear anything?"

"I didn't," said Nick. "You see, once I let the group into the escape room, I put on my headphones to listen to a new playlist Zoey sent me."

"How did the people get out of the room?" asked Henry.

"Oh! I felt them banging on the door," said Nick. "I let them out, and they ran out of here like a ghost was after them. That's when Maru pulled up."

"Why didn't you go outside and ask what was going on?" asked Violet.

"I heard them yelling about it," said Nick. "I was

too embarrassed to talk to Maru. I'm sure I'm fired now."

"She'll probably understand," said Violet. "But this was very bad for her business."

"We should check outside," said Jessie. "Maybe there are clues out there about what the group heard."

"As long as we stay together," said Benny.

"Of course," said Henry, mussing Benny's hair. "Let's go."

Henry opened the back door, and they all headed into the yard. As the children were walking around the corner, Violet tripped. Jessie caught her just in time.

"Look," said Violet. "A bone!"

There wasn't just one bone. There were dozens. They seemed to be forming a path toward the graveyard.

"Some of the skeletons lost their bones while they were marching!" said Benny.

"Oh Benny," said Jessie. "That doesn't even make sense. Remember? In the story, the skeletons only came out at night. The sun is barely setting."

Benny thought about this. Jessie had a good point. "But how else could the bones have gotten here?" he asked.

"Wait a minute," Henry said. He noticed something strange about one of the bones. He rolled it over with his foot. "There's a sticker on this one!"

"It's a barcode," said Jessie. "This is a dog bone treat!"

"So, they aren't from the graveyard?" asked Benny.

"No," said Henry. "They're just like the ones we buy from the pet store for Watch."

"Someone put them here to scare people," said Violet.

Henry snapped his fingers. "We saw Burke and Hannibal going into the pet store today," he said. "Maybe we can find out what they were doing there!"

The children headed back to the porch, where Maru was loading things into her truck.

"I was just coming to get you," she said. "Let's get out of here. I already sent Nick home."

"Okay," said Henry. "We'll change our clothes, and then we have an errand of our own to run."

* * *

"Oh look, puppies!" said Benny. "This one looks like Watch."

The children crowded around a playpen where five puppies romped around.

"Those puppies are rescues," said a voice behind them. A short woman with kind eyes appeared from the back room of the pet store. "Would you like to hold one?" she asked.

"Yes, please!" said Violet.

The woman picked up a squirming puppy and put it in Violet's arms. The puppy immediately began to lick Violet on the face.

"Stop! Stop!" Violet closed her eyes and giggled.

"It would be fun to have a friend for Watch," said Benny. He stroked the puppy's head.

"I think Watch would get jealous," said Jessie, laughing.

"You are probably right," said Violet. She handed the wiggly puppy back to the woman, who returned it to the playpen.

"What can I do for you young people?" she asked.

"We are wondering if you sell large dog bone treats," said Henry.

"Oh, of course!" said the woman. "Follow me."

She showed the children a shelf full of bones, from small to gigantic. Violet noticed that most of them had little stickers like the one they found behind the Skeleton Key.

"This one looks like a dinosaur bone," said Benny, holding up a bone almost as big as himself.

"I don't have dinosaur bones," chuckled the woman. "But I do sell a lot of the big bones. People like them for their big dogs."

"Have you sold many recently?" asked Jessie.

"Oh yes, I have," said the woman. "Do you know Burke? The graveyard keeper? He was just in with his dog, Hannibal. He bought quite a number." She shook her head slightly.

"Did that seem odd to you?" asked Henry.

"Burke? Oh, not really," said the woman. "His dog is always going through bones. He has great teeth for such an old-timer. The strange thing, now that you mention it, is Farmer Dawson. He bought more bones than any dog could go through in a whole year. I didn't even know he had a dog!"

"Maybe he just got one," said Violet.

"Well, that could be," the woman said. "But he hasn't bought any pet food or leashes. I suppose they might be for decoration for that Halloween-themed corn maze of his."

The children looked at one another. They hadn't seen any dogs at the farm. Why was Farmer Dawson buying so many bones?

"Did you want to buy one?" the woman asked.

"No, thank you," said Jessie. "We were just curious about them."

"Well, I wish I could be of more help," said the woman. "But if that's all, I need to close up the shop for the day."

The children thanked the woman for her help. They had not bought anything, but they had found just what they were looking for.

Noises in the Dark

As the children walked back to Verónica's house, they went over what they had learned.

"Those bones were just like the ones we found behind the Skeleton Key," said Violet. "I saw the stickers."

"Plus, both Burke *and* Farmer Dawson bought them," said Henry. "The question is, which one put them there?"

"I wouldn't rule out Nick just yet," said Jessie. "Every time Maru leaves, something bad seems to happen at her business. He might be involved somehow."

"Maybe," said Violet. She still did not want to think Nick was the culprit. "Whoever it is *does* seem to know just when Maru comes and goes."

"And they can get inside," said Benny. "How does that work?"

"I think I have an idea about that," said Violet. "Do you remember what that fake bank robber said at the town fair?"

"Free candy?" asked Benny.

Jessie chuckled. "I think she means the *other* thing the robbers said."

"He said that any door can be opened with the right tools," said Henry.

"That's right," said Violet. She pulled out the piece of metal she had found in the grass behind the Skeleton Key. "What if the person doesn't have a key at all? What if someone was using tools to break in?"

"I see," said Jessie. "It's not a carving tool. It's a tool to pick a lock!"

"Those are old doors in that house," said Henry. "I bet it wouldn't be too hard to pick the lock."

"But how do we find out who's doing it?" asked Benny.

"Well, we know that whoever it is likes to come

when Maru isn't there," said Jessie. "What if when Maru leaves, we stay and wait for them?"

"You mean like a stakeout?" said Benny. "In that old house? At night?"

Jessie nodded. "We know it's either Nick or Burke or Farmer Dawson. This way, if they come, we'll be waiting for them."

Benny wrung his hands. It was not Nick or Burke or Farmer Dawson that he was worried about.

***

The children laid out their sleeping bags on the floor of the Skeleton Key lobby.

"Anything else you children need for your campout?" asked Maru. The Aldens had not told Maru they were staying in the house to try to catch their culprit. They did not want to worry her any more than she already was.

"I think we have everything we need," said Henry.

"Well, don't stay up telling ghost stories too late," said Maru. "If you need anything, let me know. I'm just down the road."

As soon as Maru left, the children turned off the

lights and went to the windows.

"If the culprit is keeping a close eye on the Skeleton Key, they would have seen Maru's red truck drive away," said Henry. He and Violet looked out the front windows, while Jessie and Benny looked out the back. For a while, it was quiet.

Before long, Benny slouched down. "Maybe they went to sleep," he said.

"Let's give it a few more minutes," said Jessie.

"Shh," Violet hushed them from the front. "I think I hear something."

Out the window, she watched a lone figure walk slowly up to the house. It was dark, and she could not make out what the person was wearing.

The children gathered around the front door with their flashlights ready. Slowly, footsteps creaked up the front porch. The door handle jiggled.

"Get ready," Henry whispered.

The door swung open, but before the children could turn on their flashlights, the intruder turned on the light.

"Nick!" said Violet.

The young man jumped when he saw the children standing in front of him. "What are you all doing here?" he asked.

"We are trying to figure out who has been causing problems for the Skeleton Key," said Henry. "The question is, what are *you* doing here?"

Nick sighed. "I felt so bad about everything that's happened lately. I came back to make sure Maru locked up. She was pretty upset when she sent me home earlier."

Nick looked around at all the decorations. "She worked so hard on this," he said. "And I didn't do enough to help her like I promised."

"You've been spending a lot of time with Zoey and your band," said Jessie.

Nick nodded. "Zoey has been keeping me busy. She says I shouldn't be working for Maru."

"Zoey doesn't like you working at the Skeleton Key?" asked Henry.

"Not at all," Nick said. "She thinks it's a waste of time."

"She seemed to know all about it when we talked to her," said Violet. "Did you tell her about what we were doing to get it ready?"

"Um, no, not really," said Nick. "Like I said, she thinks it's a waste of time."

Henry looked at Nick. He wondered how Zoey knew so much about the Skeleton Key if she hadn't been told, since she'd never been inside.

Nick shook his head sadly. "Now I don't know how to make it up to Maru," he said. "I guess I should go home."

"Did you walk here?" asked Henry.

"Yeah," said Nick. "I live just up the road a little." He pulled a flashlight from his back pocket and flipped it on.

"We'll see you later," said Violet.

"Okay," said Nick. "Be sure to lock up when you leave." He waved and walked out the door.

"Nick seemed pretty worried about Maru," said Violet. "I don't think he's the one we're looking for."

"I think he's telling the truth too," said Henry.

"Well, I don't think we're going to find out anything more tonight," said Jessie. "Why don't we lock up and get to sleep?"

"Good idea," said Benny. Even with the

excitement, he was ready to curl up in his warm sleeping bag. But just as the children turned out the lights, they heard another noise. This time, it came from the backyard.

Crunch, crunch. Crunch, crunch.

"It's the marching skeletons!" cried Benny.

"Whatever it is, we should investigate," said Henry. "Come on, and stick together!"

Violet gave Henry her flashlight, and they headed outside toward the sound. They walked for a long time before they found themselves outside the wooden gate by the toolshed.

"The noise is coming from by the shed," whispered Violet. They peered through the slats in the gate and saw a light. The sound was much louder now.

Crunch, crunch. Crunch, crunch.

"Look, it's Burke!" said Jessie. "It looks like he's digging a hole."

The sound was coming from Burke's shovel hitting the dirt. On the ground, near where Burke was digging, was a pile of bones.

"A skeleton!" cried Benny.

Burke looked up and spotted the children on the other side of the gate. "What are you kids doing here?" he asked.

"What are you doing with that skeleton?" said Benny.

"Oh, for pity's sake," said Burke. "Come in. This is not a skeleton."

Jessie tugged the gate open, and the children ventured to where Burke was standing. They could see that the bones next to the hole were the same kind they saw in the store.

"Why are you burying dog bones?" asked Violet.

"I am not burying any bones," said Burke. "I'm digging them up!"

"Who buried them?" asked Jessie.

"Who else?" said Burke. "Hannibal, of course. Over all these years of taking care of the graveyard, he's gotten used to being outside. He likes it so much, I built him a doghouse next to the shed there." He pointed to a structure nearby.

"I spoiled him too much. Now he goes around burying the bones I buy for him. He likes to have a stash close to his house, so he buries them here."

"And you dig them up? Why?" asked Henry.

"They're right in front of the toolshed! The ground is so uneven from all his digging, I can't even pull my lawnmower out of the shed," said Burke. "It's a never-ending task."

"We found a bunch of dog bones behind the Skeleton Key," said Jessie. "Did Hannibal put them there?"

"Hannibal? No, I don't let him out of the graveyard," said Burke. "Probably those kids from town. When I lived in that house, kids would come around at all hours. They would dare each other to run up at night and ring the doorbell. They would also sneak into the graveyard, until I left Hannibal in here to keep them away."

"We don't know who it is," said Violet. "Did you see anyone hanging around there today?"

"No, I was in town most of the day," said Burke. "I had to get more bones for my dog!"

Just then Hannibal came bursting into the light, yellow eyes flickering. He eyed the children and wagged his big black tail.

"Speak of the devil!" said Burke. He patted

Hannibal on the head fondly as the dog sniffed at the pile of bones. Hannibal picked one up and put it down. Then he picked up another, like he couldn't choose which one he wanted. "Yeah, you'll be burying these again tonight. I can count on that!" Burke chuckled.

Henry saw that Burke loved his dog and didn't have anything to do with the problems at the Skeleton Key. "That explains the stories about the skeletons and about Hannibal," said Henry. "But who was playing the mean tricks on the Skeleton Key?"

The children were about to get their answer.

CHAPTER 10

Clattering Bones

"Look," said Violet. "Headlights!"

The children watched as, in the distance, a vehicle pulled up next to the Skeleton Key. They heard a car door slam.

"Let's go!" said Henry.

The Aldens hurried back to the Skeleton Key, and Jessie sent a text message to Maru, telling her to come right away.

As Henry, Jessie, Violet, and Benny approached the house, Maru parked and joined them on the driveway. Quietly, the group headed toward the front porch. The door was ajar.

"This was locked when we left," whispered Henry. "Somebody else must have unlocked it."

Benny held tight to Maru's hand.

"There are plenty of us. Let's see if we can catch whoever it is," whispered Jessie.

They slowly crept through the front door. Violet shined her flashlight around the room.

"There's nobody in here," she whispered.

A creaking noise came from the other room. "That's the sound of the coffin opening!" whispered Benny. He grabbed Jessie's hand.

"Let's check it out," said Henry. He pushed open the door to the escape room, and everyone crowded in.

"There's a skeleton in the corner!" yelled Benny.

The skeleton tried to clatter to the open door, but Jessie slammed it shut. "Turn on the light!" she cried.

Maru flipped a hidden switch, and the room lit up. The skeleton clattered backward as another figure leapt from behind the coffin. The two bumped into each other and fell to the floor.

"Farmer Dawson!" said Violet. "What are you doing in here?"

"And who is that, holding up your grinning

skeleton?" asked Henry. The figure took off its face mask.

"Zoey!" said Jessie.

"I think you two owe me an explanation," said Maru. "It appears you have been sabotaging my business."

Farmer Dawson looked at everyone, then hung his head. "I don't know where to begin."

"I think we can help," said Jessie. "You were upset that Maru was opening a business next door, so you decided to try to ruin her business."

"You broke in using a lock pick," said Violet. She held up the tool she had found behind the house. "And you tried to scare people into believing the stories about the house were true."

"And once you saw how the Skeleton Key worked, you took the idea of using riddles and used it for your corn maze," said Henry.

Farmer Dawson sighed. "It's all true," he said.

"The chalkboard?" asked Maru.

"That was me," said Zoey sheepishly.

"The noises outside?" asked Maru.

"It was both of us," said Zoey. "The first time,

we scratched the window with branches. Then we used a can of nails to make the marching sound."

Maru looked around the room at all of the things she had worked so hard on. "How did you know when I wasn't here?"

"Yes," said Jessie. "You must have been watching the house closely."

"That was easy," said Zoey. "I could see your comings and goings from the hot-air balloon. When I saw your cherry-red truck drive away, I'd just text my dad. Then he'd go over."

"That's why you were texting so much in the hot-air balloon!" said Violet.

"And I knew where Nick was too, since he is in my band," Zoey continued. "I just kept him busy when I needed him out of the way. I even sent him music to listen to when Dad was about to scare off that last group you had here."

"That was quite the plan," said Maru. "So I guess the last question is why. Why did you want to hurt my business?"

Violet noticed that Maru was shaking. She took her hand.

"I didn't exactly want to destroy it," said Farmer Dawson. "It's just that I was mad that you opened up right next door!"

"We were afraid you were trying to take away our customers. Our farm festival has been around forever," said Zoey.

"I had no intention of trying to hurt your business," said Maru. "I felt we would both benefit by having something unique in town. Two attractions are better than one, right?"

"Yeah," said Benny. "We like corn mazes and mystery rooms."

"I had no idea," said Farmer Dawson, "and I am truly sorry. I was being very selfish, and I want to make things right with us."

"That will take a lot of work," said Maru. "But you can start by not stealing ideas. Instead, we can work together."

Zoey looked at her father. "We would like that," she said. "I have to admit, you had some great ideas."

"I know!" said Benny. "You could put a bunch of skeletons between the farm and the Skeleton Key. They could help point the way."

Everyone laughed at the thought of such a sight along the road.

"Maybe someday," said Maru. "But right now we need to come up with ideas to get people back to the Skeleton Key tomorrow."

"I can make flyers and pass them out at our town fair," said Zoey.

"And I will tell everyone who comes to the maze to head on over here," promised Farmer Dawson.

"All right," said Maru. "Well, it's a start. I'm exhausted. Let's call it a night, shall we?" She turned the knob on the door so everyone could leave.

"Oh dear," she said.

"What is it?" asked Benny.

"I guess we are going to have to start working together sooner than I thought," said Maru. "I left the key on the desk!"

**Read on for a
sneak preview of**

SCIENCE FAIR
SABOTAGE

**the new
Boxcar Children mystery!**

"My arms are tired." Six-year-old Benny Alden set his paddle across his legs. "I don't want to row anymore."

"Benny, we need your paddle in the water to keep the canoe straight," said Henry from the back of the boat. At fourteen, he was the oldest of the four children. "You're an important part of Team Alden."

Still, Benny didn't put his paddle in the water.

Jessie spoke up from her seat in the front of the canoe. She was twelve and always seemed to know just what to tell her little brother. "This is the roughest patch of the river, Benny. Remember, there's a big meal waiting at the end."

At the mention of food, Benny pushed his sweat-soaked hair from his forehead. He flexed his muscles and said, "I'll do it for Team Alden!"

But before Benny could do a thing, the river's

current pulled the canoe sideways.

"Watch out!" Ten-year-old Violet called. She had been taking pictures of the scenery with her new digital camera. Now, she picked up her paddle.

Ahead, a glistening boulder stuck high out of the water. If the children didn't steer around it, the canoe would flip and dump them all into the river.

"Smash alert!" Benny shrieked. "Crash position!" He ducked down and put his head between his legs.

"No need to panic. We just need to paddle together," Henry said. He called, "Stroke! Stroke! Stroke!" The three oldest Aldens worked double time to turn the boat back on course. Before long, the rock was behind them.

"Whew," said Violet, smoothing out her ponytail. "That was close."

"I was so scared!" said Benny. Then he added, "I think we all deserve a snack. Is there a cooler hiding somewhere?"

"Sorry," Henry said. "This is a short trip, remember? Grandfather is waiting for us."

It was a late summer day, and the children were enjoying the last of the warm weather by canoeing down the Greenfield River. At the end of their route, they planned to meet Grandfather for lunch at Greenfield's Lookout Café.

"How much longer, Henry?" Benny asked. He added, "Do you have a sandwich in your life jacket pocket?"

"Life jackets don't have pockets, silly," Henry chuckled.

Violet pulled the straps to tighten the orange vest around her middle. "It's good we were wearing life jackets," she said. "We almost tipped over."

"It's important to be prepared," said Henry. "Sometimes things happen that no one can control."

"It's important to be prepared," Benny repeated. He thought for a long moment then said, "I think I'll make a life jacket with a special pocket for a sandwich." He added, "I'm going to invent a machine that rows the boat for me too." He went on, "Then, we need an air conditioning umbrella to cool us down. A waterproof boat pillow to rest my sleepy head." Benny's eyes got big as he added another idea to the list. "And a special doggy seat for Watch!"

Watch was the name of the Aldens' wirehaired

terrier. The man who rented the canoe to them had said no dogs were allowed. So Watch was waiting with Grandfather at the end of the route.

Benny had been upset not to bring Watch along. Now, he was excited about his idea. "I could make a doggy life vest too!" He clapped his hands. "With a pocket for dog treats!"

"You are full of good ideas," said Jessie. "Maybe I should use one for my science fair project."

All summer, Jessie had been looking forward to joining her school's Science Fair Club. In the club's first meeting, she had partnered with Claudia Tobin, who had won the competition the year before. Jessie was excited to have such a smart partner. Now, they just needed to find the perfect project.

"You're going to invent a dog life vest, Jessie?" Violet asked, brown eyes wide with surprise.

"With a treat pocket," Benny added. "That's the most important part."

Jessie giggled. "I don't think Claudia would want to make a dog vest."

"You've only had one meeting," Henry said.

"The perfect idea will come to you."

For a few minutes, the children were quiet as they paddled around a bend. Henry convinced Benny to help by promising him *two* sandwiches at the end of the trip.

"And ice cream?" Benny asked before putting his oar into the water.

"I'd never forget dessert," said Henry.

Before long, the children came to a calm area where they could float along. Violet took a picture of a mallard duck that Benny spotted. And two turtles Henry pointed out.

But Jessie was still thinking about her science fair project. "Claudia and I want to do something that will make a difference," she said. "We have to decide soon so we can get busy doing the research."

"You'll find your project," said Benny. "I'm a hundred and two percent positive."

"I've got my fingers crossed one hundred and two times," Jessie joked.

"It's nice we have this river and so much nature this close to Greenfield," said Violet, peering through her camera lens. "Maybe there's a river project you could do, Jessie?"

"I wonder..." Jessie began to think about it.

Violet aimed her camera toward the shore and squinted through the lens. "Hey, what's going on over there?"

"What do you see?" asked Henry.

"It looks like construction," Violet said.

As the boat got closer, the children saw a tall metal fence blocking off the work site from the river. Loud clanging noises came from the other side.

"That's strange," said Jessie. "I didn't think anyone could build by the river—not after the Big Cleanup."

"Big Cleanup?" Benny asked.

"That's right," said Henry. "Awhile back, there was a big effort to clean the Greenfield River. At the time, there were no birds. The water smelled weird. Everyone used to joke there was so much pollution in the river that the fish had three eyes."

"Mutant fish!" said Benny. He peeked over the side of the canoe to see if he could find any strange creatures. "I thought falling in the water would be bad. Swimming with mutant fishes would be..." He thought about the right word, then said, "Really bad!"

"Those are just rumors, Benny." Jessie pointed to a fishing dock on the side of the river, where a man and his daughter were holding fishing rods. The girl had a fish hanging from a hook. "See? Nothing to worry about."

"Don't eat that!" Benny shouted. "It might have extra eyeballs!"

"We need to paddle," said Henry, changing the subject. The end of the river ride was coming up, and the children needed to get to the right side of the riverbank. "All together, Team Alden! Stroke. Stoke. Stroke."

Still, as Jessie paddled along, she couldn't help but look at the water and wonder: Had things really changed for the Greenfield River?

GERTRUDE CHANDLER WARNER discovered when she was teaching that many readers who like an exciting story could find no books that were both easy and fun to read. She decided to try to meet this need, and her first book, *The Boxcar Children*, quickly proved she had succeeded.

Miss Warner drew on her own experiences to write the mystery. As a child she spent hours watching trains go by on the tracks opposite her family home. She often dreamed about what it would be like to set up housekeeping in a caboose or freight car—the situation the Alden children find themselves in.

While the mystery element is central to each of Miss Warner's books, she never thought of them as strictly juvenile mysteries. She liked to stress the Aldens' independence and resourcefulness and their solid New England devotion to using up and making do. The Aldens go about most of their adventures with as little adult supervision as possible—something else that delights young readers.

Miss Warner lived in Putnam, Connecticut, until her death in 1979. During her lifetime, she received hundreds of letters from girls and boys telling her how much they liked her books.